For Hannah, Elizabeth, and Oliver

The Wonderful

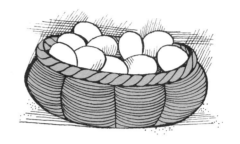

Eggs of Furicchia

A Picture Story From Italy

Written and Illustrated by Anne Rockwell

The World Publishing Company, Cleveland and New York

A Note About the Story

In the days of the Italian Renaissance the witch, or *strega*, was called upon frequently for her services by respectable people, and many a poor widow turned to the art of enchantment to make a comfortable living. She sold mysterious love potions, charms which made crops grow, and various cures for the ailments of both people and livestock. A *strega* was also the heiress to a great amount of folklore, much of which may have survived from Etruscan times in Tuscany.

The story of Furicchia is about a pleasant and gracious *strega* living in the city of Florence in the early fifteenth century. The original story, adapted in this picture book, was collected by a nineteenth-century German folklorist, Hans Breitmann, from a Florentine *strega* who was, at that time, doing a thriving business, and who knew by heart many of the ancient charms, songs, and stories in the old Tuscan dialect.

Published by The World Publishing Company, 2231 West 110th Street, Cleveland, Ohio 44102. Published simultaneously in Canada by Nelson, Foster & Scott Ltd. Library of Congress catalog card number: 69-13050. Copyright © 1969 by Anne Rockwell. All rights reserved. No part of this book may be reproduced in any form without written permission from the publisher, except for brief passages included in a review appearing in a newspaper or magazine. Printed in the United States of America. Typography by Jack Jaget.

Long ago, in the city of Florence, there stood a little shop
where an old lady named Furicchia sold eggs.

And what eggs they were! Although they were ordinary
looking—and even a little smaller than some—

wonderful things began to happen to those who ate them.

Sick children became
strong and healthy;

plain girls became pretty;
timid young men grew bold;

shepherds lost none of their sheep;

all of the figs ripened on farmers' trees; travelers
met with no robbers on their journeys;

and a few fools even
became wise men—all
from eating the wonder-
ful eggs of Furicchia!

But there was a strange thing about Furicchia's eggs. No
one had ever seen her buy them from a farmer in the
market place, as all the other egg-women in the city did.
And yet, she always had more eggs than anyone else;
even in the times when the hens refused to lay and eggs

grew scarce, Furicchia had more than enough to supply her many customers. People agreed that she must be a witch to produce these enchanted eggs from nowhere—but since her charms brought only good, everyone loved her and she grew quite prosperous from her egg shop.

That is to say, everyone loved her but one. She had a neighbor called Maddalena who, besides being mean and selfish, was far from beautiful, and while she was not poor, neither was she rich. She envied Furicchia her good fortune and grew to hate her. The reason was this:

When Maddalena had seen the
wonderful things that happened
to those who ate Furicchia's eggs,

she thought that if she ate one,
she would, no doubt, become
beautiful and rich. But when she
asked to buy a dozen eggs,
Furicchia said:

"Keep your money, Maddalena. These eggs, I am sorry to say, would do you no good. For they are only a help to those with a kind heart. For anyone else, I am afraid, they are no better than other eggs; in fact, they are even a little smaller and less tasty than most!"

But Maddalena insisted, and so Furicchia sold her a dozen eggs. Each day Maddalena ate one. She ate them hard-boiled; she ate them in omelets—but even so, after nearly two weeks she was not a bit more beautiful, nor was she rich. Nothing at all had changed, except that perhaps, if this was possible, her bad temper had grown even worse. She decided that Furicchia had tricked her, and she hated her more each day. She became determined to discover the secret of Furicchia's eggs and to steal it from her.

The secret was this:
Many years earlier, kindhearted Furicchia
had rescued a poor little black-and-white
hen from the butcher just as he was about
to make her ready for the soup pot.

Now this hen was a magic one; she needed
only to be fed a special broth and then she
would lay, each night, dozens and dozens
of her wonderful eggs. She taught Furicchia
the recipe for this magic broth and Furicchia made it carefully and lovingly for the
little hen. Each year the hen grew more and
more magnificent, until her feathers spar-
kled like stars in the sky and her eyes and
beak grew bright and golden as the sun.

But all day she stayed hidden in the darkest corner of Furicchia's cupboard, and only at night, while the city slept, did she come out. Then she would drink her broth and, clucking gaily, she would dance about and begin to lay her eggs.

One day Furicchia closed her shop and headed for the hills

to take some eggs to a farmer whose donkey was sick.

As she expected it would be nighttime before she returned,
she mixed her hen's broth before she left—
a little wine;
a little lemon juice;

some olives from a tree where
an owl-chick lived;

one ripe fig, picked at
the full moon;

a dried petal from a January-blooming rose;

an onion ;

three pinches of gold dust ; and a tiny
sprinkling of powder from a butterfly's wing.

While she mixed the ingredients Furicchia
sang a little song the hen had taught her,
with words no one else could understand.
Then, when the broth was well mixed, she
set it on the fire to simmer, locked the door,
and went on her way.

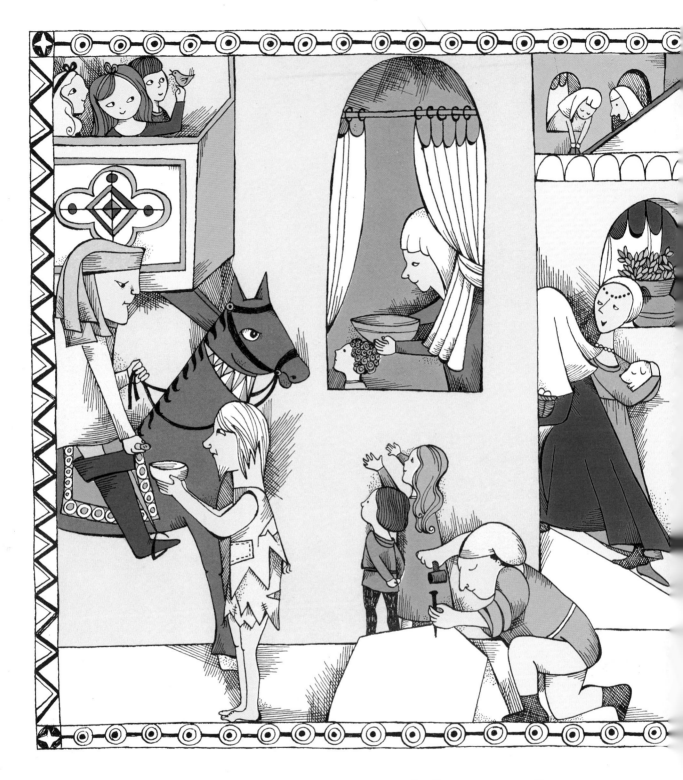

No sooner had Furicchia turned the corner than
Maddalena climbed in through an open window.

At last her chance had come to discover
Furicchia's secret!

When she entered the egg shop, she saw no eggs (for the shop was closed for business that day), but only the broth simmering gently on the fire. How good it smelled! How tasty it looked! And so, Maddalena helped herself to a spoonful. It was so delicious and so unlike anything that she had ever tasted before she felt certain this broth was the thing that brought good fortune to Furicchia's customers. Deciding that this was so, she drank it all up, and left the way she came. The hen, who had watched her all this time through a crack in the cupboard, chuckled to herself.

As soon as Maddalena looked in her mirror, she knew that she had been right! She looked a little different— her eyes were brighter and more sparkling than she had ever seen them—and she felt a little different too, although it was hard to say just how.

Furicchia returned home much sooner than she had expected, for the donkey had recovered rapidly—the moment, in fact, that he had barely tasted one egg.

When Maddalena saw Furicchia coming down the street, she rushed out to tell her of her triumph!

But when she began to call to her, the only sound that she could make was:

"Cluck, Cluck!...Cluck, Cluck!
Cluck, Cluck, Cluck!"

And then Maddalena saw that she had grown small —
very, very small...about the size of a hen...in fact, she
was a hen, although not such a pretty one as Furicchia's.

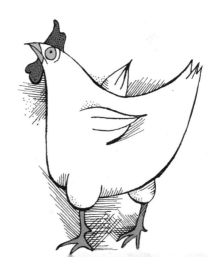

And, sad to say, the eggs that she laid from that day forth were not so wonderful as those of Furicchia's hen —although they were unusual, for when they hatched, out came, not chicks...

but mice, and they all ran away!

J